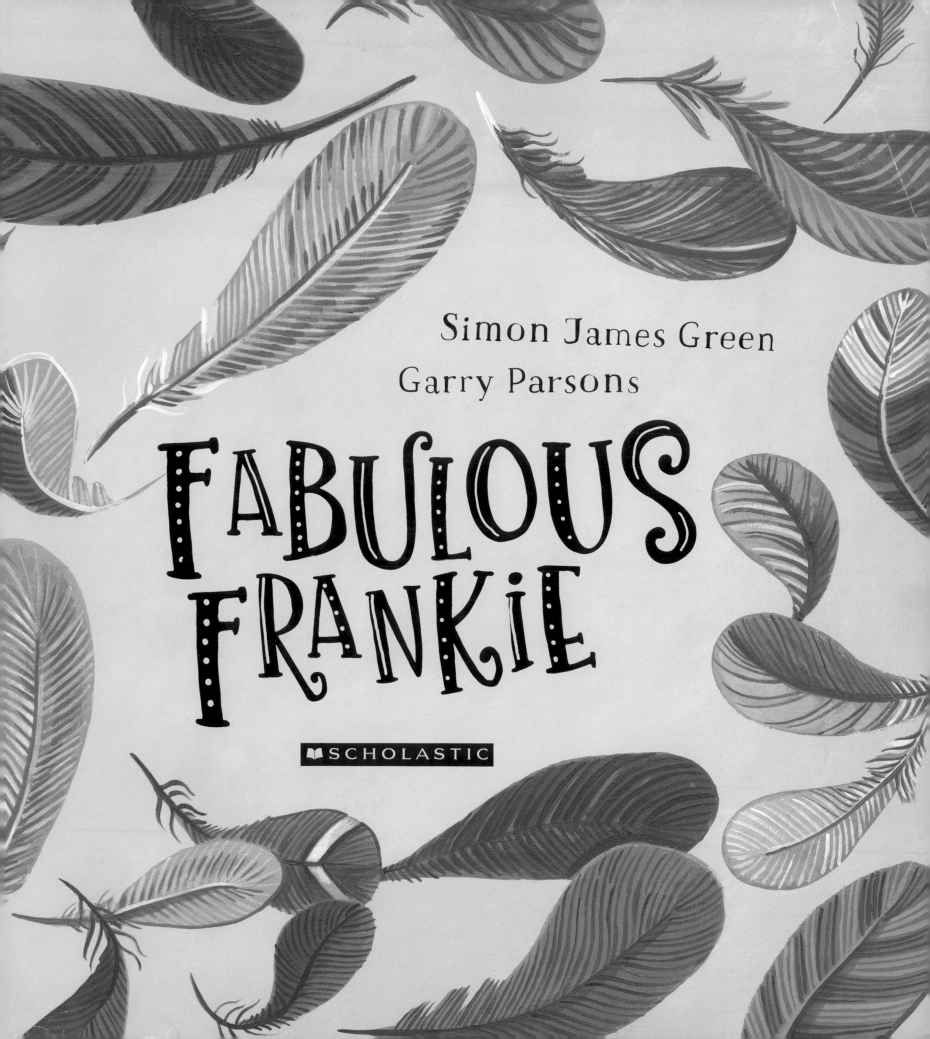

Simon James Green

Garry Parsons

FABULOUS FRANKIE

SCHOLASTIC

If there was one thing Frankie loved more than being a flamingo, it was being

FABULOUS.

He had bright, pink feathers –
FABULOUS.

He had
FABULOUS
long legs.

And the only word to
describe his elegant
neck would be
'FABULOUS'.

But there
was one
problem...

Everyone else was fabulous too!
How would he ever stand out
and be *truly* fabulous?

Luckily,
Frankie had a plan.
A FABULOUS plan.

Frankie got to work, sewing.

"Sequins, sequins and MORE sequins!"

he sang.

Soon his new outfit was done – it glimmered, it shimmered, it shone!

Frankie couldn't wait for the others to see him – he'd really stand out now.

He performed a flawless *grande jeté* into the crowd. "TA DAH!"

... Oh.

Well that's bitterly disappointing!
Frankie thought. *I don't look
special AT ALL!*

Then he spotted a sign.
"Aha!" said Frankie.

Frankie bought the most
BEAUTIFUL fan he could find,
made from the finest silks.

"Oh, this little thing?
It's only my fan!" said Frankie,
sashaying into the lagoon.

"So EYE-CATCHING, no? You might say

FANTABULOUS!"

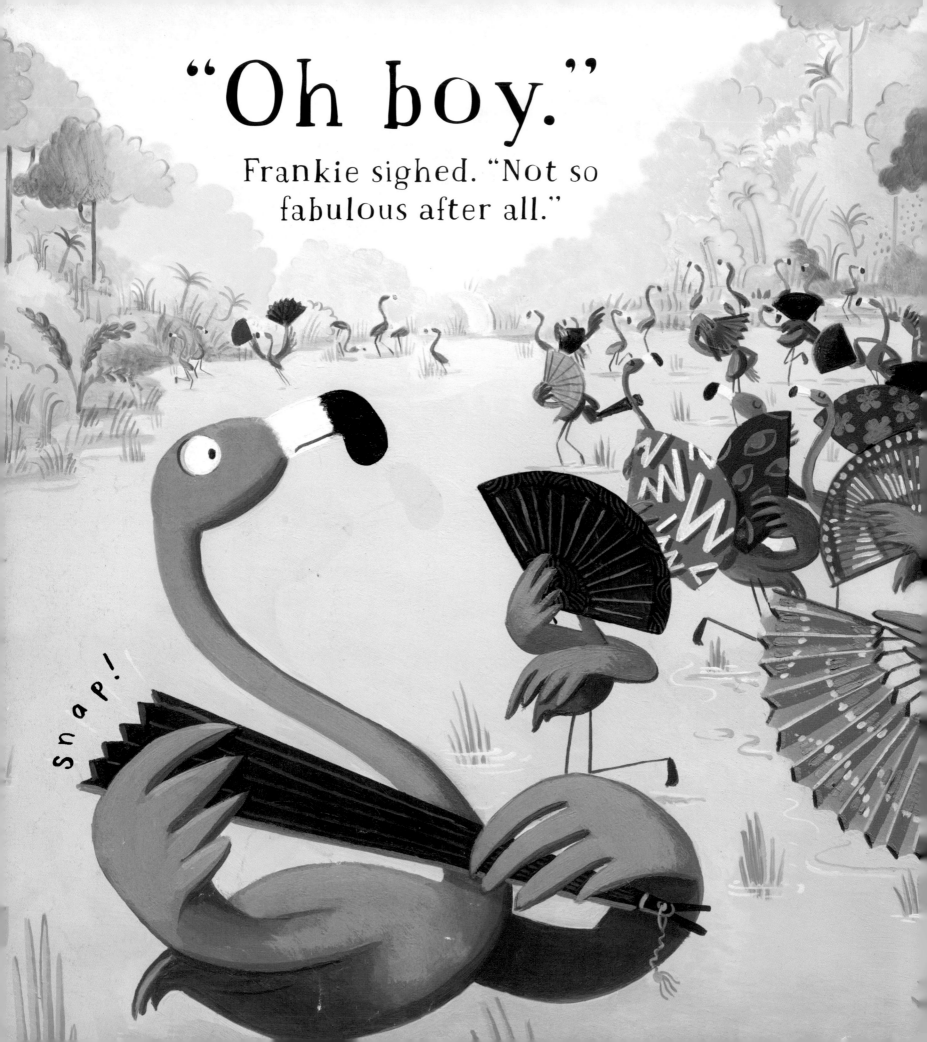

"Right," muttered Frankie. "If there's one thing guaranteed to be fabulous, it's

GLITTER

and this little puppy fires it out by the bucketload!"

Oh yes you cannon

Frankie lit the fuse and stood back, ready for his most spectacular entrance yet.

"Greetings, fellow flamingoes!" he trilled.

"I'm FAB-U-LOUS!"

BOOM!

The sky filled with fabulous glitter, and Frankie waited for the applause he so richly deserved.

Frankie's flouncing soon became a tragic trudging. "Hello, Flo," he said, spotting his neighbour. "Need some help with those bags?"

"That's so kind!" Flo said.

"Well, that's all I'm good for now," he grumbled. "Plain old Frankie. Carting bags around like a common mule."

"I'M NOT COMMON!" said a passing mule.

"Oh! I'm *so* sorry, that was inexcusably rude of me!" Frankie said.

"You're helpful!" added Flo.

"And you apologise when you've hurt someone's feelings," said the mule.

Frankie was filled with a FABULOUS feeling.

It wasn't the glitz.

It wasn't the glamour.

Everyone liked him just for being himself – and that was the most fabulous thing of all!

Fab-u-lous!

Although that's not to say his pashmina wasn't fabulous too.
I mean, look at it – the orange satin detailing is perfection itself!

SJG – For Paddy
Who will always be his
own sort of fabulous

GP – For Simon

First published in 2021 by Scholastic Children's Books
Euston House, 24 Eversholt Street
London NW1 1DB, UK
A division of Scholastic Ltd
www.scholastic.co.uk

London · New York · Toronto · Sydney
Auckland · Mexico City · New Delhi · Hong Kong

ISBN 978 1407 19704 3